For William, Robin and Tom
~ H. W.

For Jess, love Aunty Bek xx
~ R. H.

tiger tales
5 River Road, Suite 128, Wilton, CT 06897
Published in the United States 2015
Originally published in Great Britain 2014
by Little Tiger Press
Text copyright © 2014 Holly Webb
Illustrations copyright © 2014 Rebecca Harry
ISBN-13: 978-1-58925-170-0
ISBN-10: 1-58925-170-9
Printed in China
LTP/1400/0986/0914
10 9 8 7 6 5 4 3 2 1

For more insight and activities,
visit us at www.tigertalesbooks.com

Little Puppy
LOST

by Holly Webb   Illustrated by Rebecca Harry

tiger tales

Harry's tail wagged as he raced through the park.
His eyes sparkled, and his ears flapped from side to side
as he looked at all the exciting things.

"Today's our first ever walk, Harry!" Emma said,
giving him a little hug. "Isn't it fun?"

Harry wriggled with happiness. The park was the
most wonderful place he had ever seen!

Suddenly, a bright red ball bounced past Harry's nose. His ears twitched as he chased after it. He was so excited, he didn't notice his brand new collar had slipped off!

"Come back!" Emma cried, waving the leash. But Harry didn't hear her.

He pounced on the ball happily. But then he heard a noise.

Staring down at Harry were two huge dogs.
Harry wriggled backward. "You can chase my ball,"
he said, in a wobbly whisper.

"Oh, no," the bigger dog barked. "We want to
chase you!"

Harry yelped and raced for
the woods. But the other dogs
started chasing him.

Harry spotted a place to hide in a large tree.
He wriggled inside just as the dogs raced by.
He waited, and waited, and waited, then at last
he poked his nose out.

"It's all right. They're gone," a voice said from high above.

Harry squeaked in surprise! Looking down at him was a thin tabby cat.

"You're too little to be out here on your own," the cat said.

"I'm lost," Harry sniffed. "And I don't know where my best friend Emma is."

"I was lost once, too," the cat smiled gently. "Don't worry, I can show you how to get out of these woods."

"Oh, thank you!" the little puppy beamed. "I'm Harry."

"And I'm Ginger!" said the cat. "Follow me!"

Harry trotted after
Ginger. Suddenly, a
huge bird flapped out
of the shadows in front
of them.

"Watch out!" Ginger
cried, as Harry
tumbled into a pile
of leaves.

"Do you mind?" snapped a grumpy-looking hedgehog.

"Come on," Ginger sighed. "Almost there."

Harry's ears pricked up happily. Emma would be so pleased to see him!

"Emma! Emma!" Harry barked. But the park was empty now, dark and silent.

"She's gone," Harry cried as he sank down on the cold grass. "I want to go home," he whimpered.

Ginger gave him a gentle nudge. "We'll find the way.
And we'll find you something to eat, too," she added,
as they set off toward the town.

"Down here?" Harry sniffed uncertainly.

The alley was dark, but something in the cans smelled delicious.

Then he heard a noise . . . .

There in the darkness was a huge white cat.
She hissed at Ginger and batted at her with
her claws.

Harry growled. There was no time to lose!
He took a deep breath, and . . .

... BARKED and BARKED and BARKED!
The noise echoed through the alley.

The white cat took off.

Ginger stared in amazement. "Harry!" she cheered. "You're a hero!"

Harry wagged his tail shyly, and sniffed around for something else to eat. But then he stopped, and his nose quivered. "Oh!" he squeaked.

"What is it?" Ginger asked.

"I can smell home!" Harry
cried as he darted out of the alley.
"It's this way!"

The two friends ran down the brightly-lit
street until . . . .

"This is my house!" Harry cried,
scratching at the front door.

"Harry!" Emma raced to scoop him up.
"You came home," she murmured,
   rubbing her cheek against his soft ears.
"We were so worried about you!"

But Harry jumped down.
He'd forgotten Ginger!
"Don't go!" he yelped.
Ginger was trailing out of
the garden, her ears drooping
and sad.
"Did you bring a friend?"
Emma whispered as Harry led
Ginger back up the path.

Emma took them inside and gave them lots to eat. Then Harry snuggled up on her lap.

"There's room for you, too," Emma whispered to Ginger.

The old cat purred happily. She curled herself around her friend, and together they fell fast asleep, home and safe at last.